BEWARE OF A VERY HUNGRY FOX

by Patty Wolcott

illustrated by Lucinda McQueen

J.B. Lippincott   New York

*"To all children
who are learning to read"*

An Addisonian Press Book

First published by Addison-Wesley Publishing Company
Beware of a Very Hungry Fox
Text copyright © 1975 by Patty Wolcott Berger
Illustrations copyright © 1975 by Lucinda McQueen
Printed in the U.S.A. All rights reserved.

Library of Congress Catalog Card Number 84-40745
ISBN 0-201-14250-3

Library of Congress Cataloging in Publication Data
Wolcott, Patty.
    Beware of a very hungry fox.
    SUMMARY: Four little chipmunks wander into a forest
thinking they are unafraid of a very hungry fox—and
then they meet one.
    "An Addisonian Press book."
    [1. Chipmunks—Fiction.   2. Foxes—Fiction]
I. McQueen, Lucinda, illus.   II. Title.
PZ7.W8185Be   [E]   74-5025
ISBN 0-201-14250-3

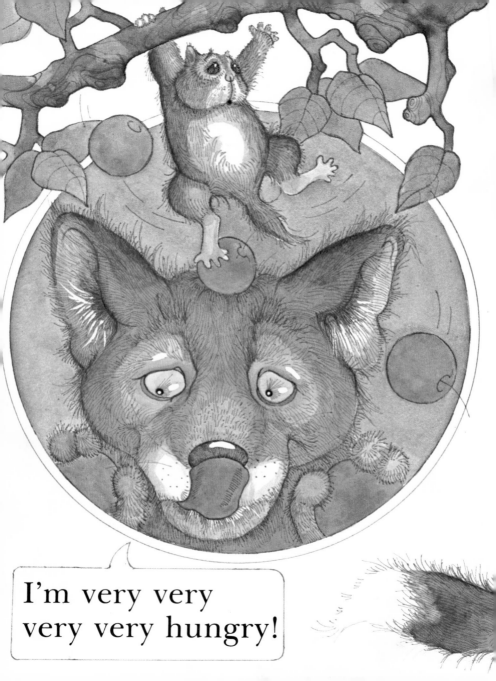

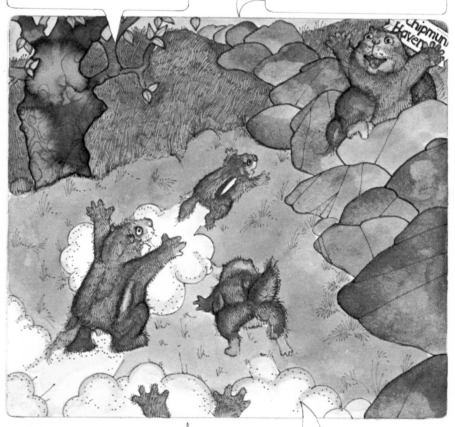

I'm hungry.
I'm very hungry.
I'm very very hungry.
I'm very very very hungry.

E